I0538114

Acknowledgements

With the greatest thanks to my heavenly Father, for allowing the miraculous formation of life and joy of motherhood.

And then to my fathers on earth: Bishop Richard and Bishop Eddy, who never laughed at me when I explained the idea, but rather laid out the realities and gave me encouragement.

To the Opare family for always believing in me. To friends who never gave up on me like, Nwamaka Ikpa and Kofi Ayeh, along with my Aberdeen family for their continued support.

And lastly, to my husband, Eric Agyei-Gyan and my girls:

Grace, Cara and Dagmar. Thank you for allowing me to be your Mummy.

© 2018 Pauline K Agyei-Gyan

When Mummy Brought Home

My Baby Sister

Can you hear
me in there,
little baby sister?

Mmmm…
or are you going to
be a mister?

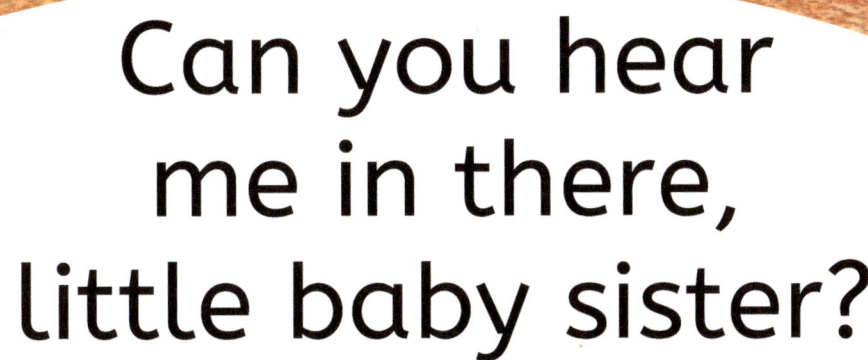

Hand on Mummy's tummy, I'm all filled with glee.

Ooo naughty naughty, you just kicked me.

When you arrive, you'll sleep beside my bed,

but for now, sleep in Mummy's tummy instead.

"Well Esther-Jean,
when they arrive you'll need
a baby's dummy

because Mummy, will surely
have a smaller tummy."

Baby basket,
Check.

Strong and steady,
Check.

Now everything is ready,
Check, Check, Check.

And there she was…
my little baby sister.

May she always be near,
so that I never miss her.

Thank you
Mummy. Thank you Daddy.
And thank you God for my
little baby sister.

Sister Emily…that Mummy
and Daddy brought safely
home to me.

Are you ready for your baby brother or sister?

Here is a checklist to help Mummy, Daddy and YOU, to get ready for the new baby!

Checklist

Items	Tick
Baby Clothes	
Nappies	
Wipes	
Bottles	
Buggy	
Cot	
Dummy	
Homemade Welcome Home Card	

www.ingramcontent.com/pod-product-compliance
Lightning Source LLC
Chambersburg PA
CBHW041610120626
46551CB00002B/380